Hide
and
Sink

The Story of Jonah

Written and Illustrated by
Damon J. Taylor

FOR PARENTS
with Dr. Sock

This story will help children learn that it's better to confess their sins than try to hide them. Here is a Scripture that you may want your child to memorize:

> *"If we confess our sins, he is faithful and just and will forgive us our sins and purify us from all unrighteousness."* (1 John 1:9)*

HERE ARE ZUM FUN ACTIVITIES FOR ZOO PARENTS TO DO VISS ZEE LITTLE KIDDIES.

Read It Together–
The story of Jonah is found in the Old Testament book of Jonah, and the fish is only part of the story!

Sharing–
Share a time when you did something that displeased your own parents and God. Your children need to know that you were once young and made mistakes too. They will be more likely to share with you after you are open with them.

Discussion Starters–
• Why did Coleman hide his disobedience?
• Has there been a time when you felt like hiding a sin?
• Who is it that sees and cares about everything we do?
• What would you do in a fish's belly for three days and nights?
• Have you ever done something you were supposed to do, even when it was something you didn't want to do? Your kids might think grown-ups never have to do things they don't want to do!
• What do you think Jonah prayed for when he was in the belly of the fish?

For Fun–
Pretend that you're Jonah sitting in the belly of the fish. Curl up in a ball and act out what you think it was like. What did it feel like? What did it smell like? Was it scary? Let your kids exercise their imagination.

Draw–
Draw with your kids. Have them draw Jonah inside the fish. Then draw yourself inside a fish. What kind of fish is it?

Prayer Time–
Thank God for always being there and caring for you, whether you obey Him or not.

COLEMAN HAS FOUND THAT THE LIFE OF A LITTLE BOY

can be tough at times, especially if that boy has a baby sister named Shelby. When Shelby was born, Coleman needed a way to deal with his day-to-day problems. He found his socks. Yes, that's right, his socks.

It may seem weird, but these aren't your regular, everyday tube socks that you find in your dresser. As ordinary as they may appear, these socks really are Coleman's friends, and they help him with his problems. When life gets complicated, Coleman goes to his bedroom and works through his troubles by playing make-believe with his socks and remembering Bible stories he's learned.

So please sit back, take off your shoes and socks if you like, and enjoy Coleman's imaginary world in . . .

Hide and Sink
The Story of Jonah

Coleman loves to play pretend with his socks. Today, he is a fighter pilot. His mother has told him time and time again not to run in the house, especially near Goldie and the fishbowl. It's a family rule. If he knocks over the fishbowl, he'll be a fighter pilot who's in *big trouble!*

Whooooosh!!! SMASH!!!

"Oh no! I've REALLY crash landed now!" thought Coleman. "Wait a minute—maybe no one heard it. Mom's at the store, and Dad is spending quality time napping with Shelby. There's only a small crack in the bowl. If I can fix it, no one will know. Hold on, Goldie!"

Coleman got his dad's duct tape, patched the crack, refilled the bowl, and dropped Goldie back into her leaky home.

"There, perfect," thought Coleman. "No one will ever know. . . ." But the more he thought about it, the more scared Coleman became.

"Mom and Dad can't punish me if they can't find me. All I have to do is hide. I am so smart!"

And Coleman knew the perfect hiding place—the clothes hamper in his bedroom.

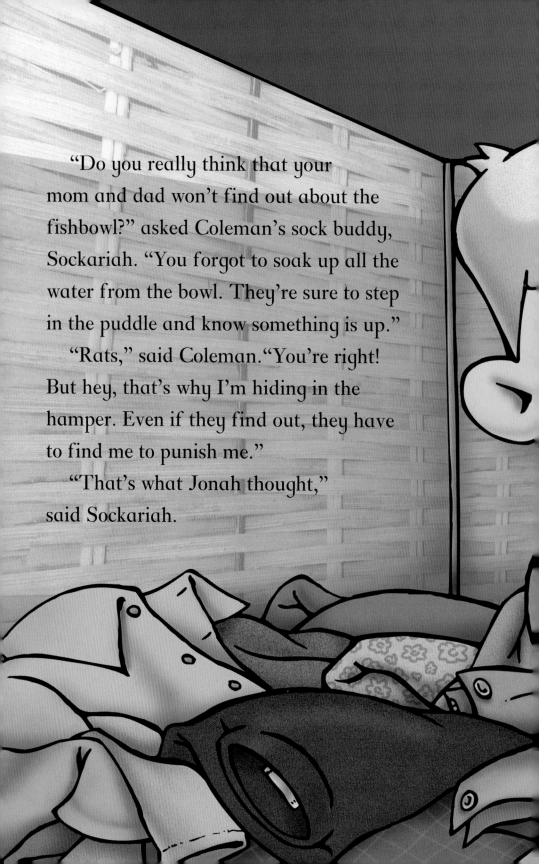

"Do you really think that your mom and dad won't find out about the fishbowl?" asked Coleman's sock buddy, Sockariah. "You forgot to soak up all the water from the bowl. They're sure to step in the puddle and know something is up."

"Rats," said Coleman. "You're right! But hey, that's why I'm hiding in the hamper. Even if they find out, they have to find me to punish me."

"That's what Jonah thought," said Sockariah.

"Who's Jonah? Did he spill his parents' fishbowl too?" asked Coleman.

"No. Don't you remember your dad reading in the Bible about that guy who tried to hide from God?" said the sock. "If not, then let me remind you. . . ."

A long time ago, in a town called Nineveh, there were many people who disobeyed God's rules. God wasn't happy about that.

God asked a man named Jonah to go to Nineveh and tell the people to change their ways, because God was very angry with them. Jonah had heard about the people of Nineveh, and he thought that they deserved to be punished for their sinfulness.

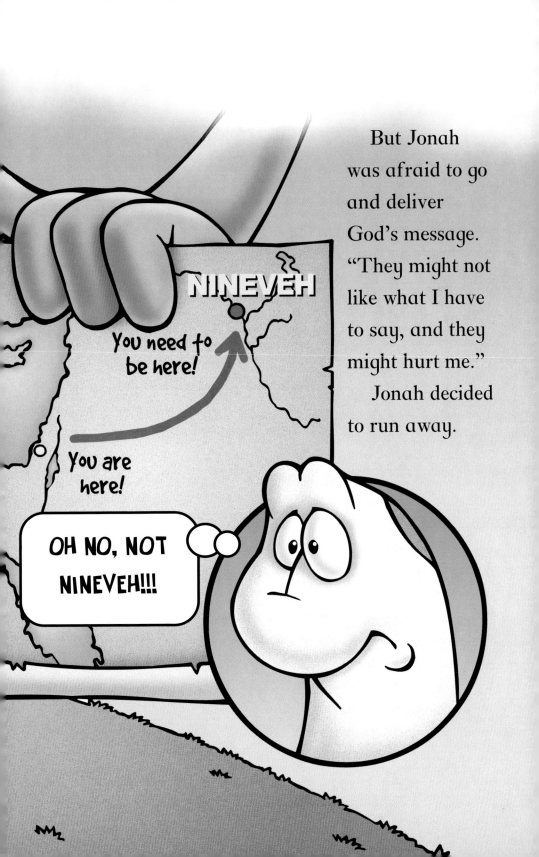

"I'm going to disguise myself and take a boat trip far from Nineveh. If I hide from God, He won't be able to find me. He can't punish me if He can't find me," thought Jonah.

"Hey, that's the same thing I thought when I knocked over the fishbowl," said Coleman.

"Oh, really?" said Sockariah. "Keep listening, and we'll see where that kind of thinking gets you."

While Jonah was hiding, he fell asleep on the lower deck of the boat.

The weather became stormy, and the tiny ship was tossed about. If it wasn't for the courage of the fearless crew, the Minnow would be wrecked. The captain of the Minnow was worried that someone on the boat had done something to upset God. He thought God had sent the storm because He was angry.

The captain went below deck to get Jonah. "Aye, Matey, me thinks you'd better wake up," called the captain to the sleeping Jonah. "Me thinks there's someone aboard who's gotten God's anger up 'n' roarin'. So we needs you to pray to your God to protect us."

Jonah knew that *someone* was himself.

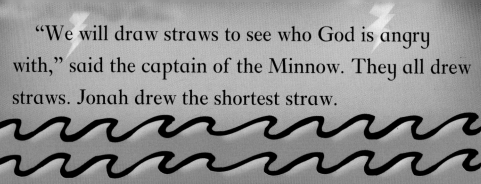

"We will draw straws to see who God is angry with," said the captain of the Minnow. They all drew straws. Jonah drew the shortest straw.

Jonah told the captain that it was Jonah himself who had disobeyed God, and that they should throw him overboard to stop the storm.

The men aboard the Minnow refused to throw Jonah overboard. The storm continued to get worse and worse.

"You *must* throw me overboard," demanded Jonah. "You will all be lost at sea if you don't!"

So the captain and his crew tossed Jonah over the side of the boat into the raging waves.

As soon as Jonah disappeared into the deep, dark sea, the waves began to settle down. Soon the storm was over.

Jonah sank deeper and deeper into what he thought would be his watery grave. But all of a sudden a great fish, which looked a lot like a giant Goldie, came from nowhere and swallowed Jonah whole.

"That's a terrible story," cried Coleman. "I may never eat fish again!"

"That's not the end of the story, Coleman. Quiet down and let me finish."

The giant fish was sent by God to protect Jonah. The fish swallowed him, but it didn't chew him up. There was just enough room and air to breathe in the belly of the fish to keep Jonah safe.

NOW THAT'S SOMETHING YOU DON'T SEE EVERY DAY.

Jonah spent three days and three nights in the fish's belly. During that time, Jonah prayed and sang praises to God for saving him from drowning. Jonah also spent time thinking about what he had done wrong.

"You mean, like he should have taken a bus instead of a boat?" asked Coleman.

"No, he thought about how foolish he had been to think that he could hide from his sin, and even more foolish to try and hide his sin from God!"

On the third day, the giant fish spat Jonah out on the beach, safe and sound. From there, Jonah went straight to Nineveh.

Jonah arrived in Nineveh and told the people to change their ways. They listened to Jonah's words from God and were ashamed. They decided to obey God, and that made God very happy.

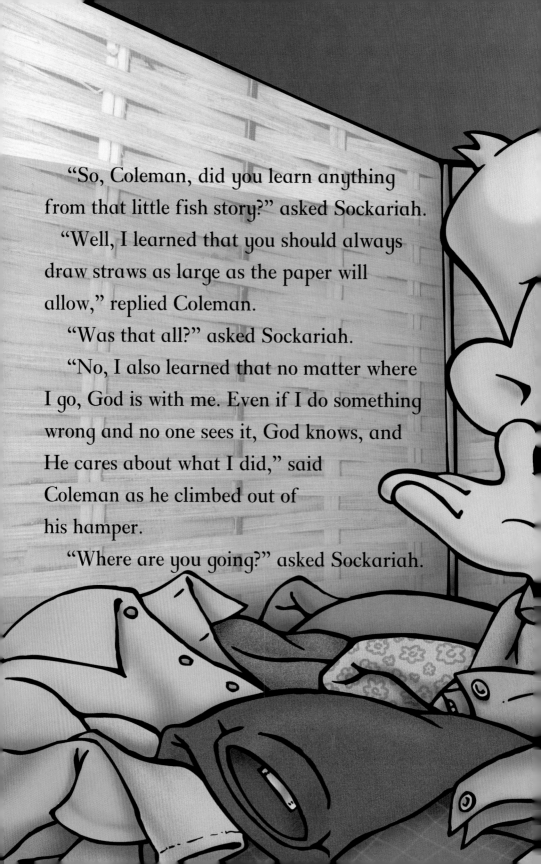

"So, Coleman, did you learn anything from that little fish story?" asked Sockariah.

"Well, I learned that you should always draw straws as large as the paper will allow," replied Coleman.

"Was that all?" asked Sockariah.

"No, I also learned that no matter where I go, God is with me. Even if I do something wrong and no one sees it, God knows, and He cares about what I did," said Coleman as he climbed out of his hamper.

"Where are you going?" asked Sockariah.

"I'm going to sit by the fishbowl and wait for Mom and Dad so I can tell them what I did." Coleman picked up a pillow and headed for the fishbowl.

Coleman waited for his mom to get home, then he told her that he had broken a rule *and* the fishbowl. Both of Coleman's parents forgave him for disobeying, but he was now a grounded fighter pilot, for breaking the fishbowl and upsetting Goldie.

And Goldie forgave Coleman, too!

The Child Sockology Series

For ages up to 5

Bible Characters A to Z
Bible Numbers 1 to 10
Bible Opposites
New Testament Bible Feelings

For ages 5 and up

The Ark and the Park: The Story of Noah
Beauty and the Booster: The Story of Esther
Forgive and Forget: The Story of Joseph
Hide and Sink: The Story of Jonah